Usborne

Big Book of Little Stories

Contents

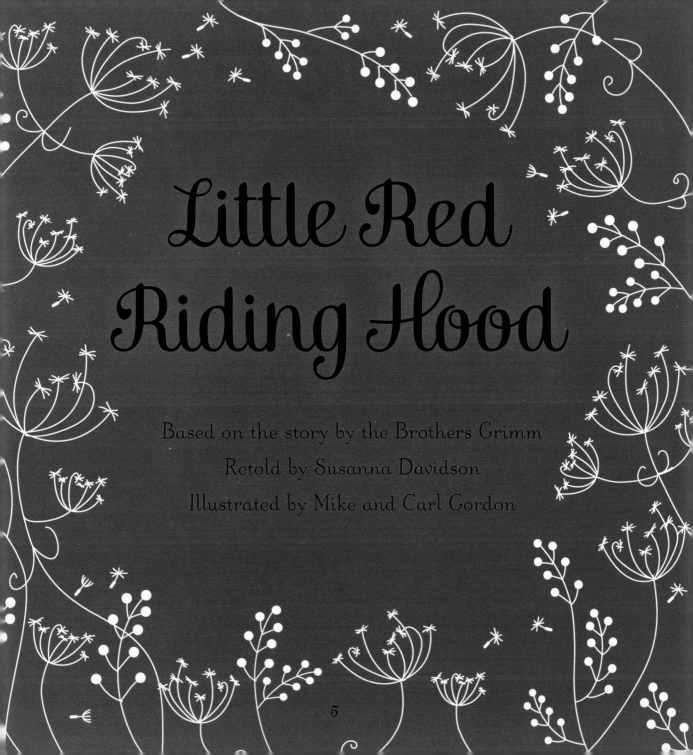

Little Red Riding Hood

Based on the story by the Brothers Grimm

Retold by Susanna Davidson

Illustrated by Mike and Carl Gordon

Once upon a time there was a little girl called Little Red Riding Hood.

She always wore a bright red cloak
with a bright red hood.

I love my cloak!

She lived with her mother in a cottage
on the edge of some deep, dark woods.

7

One day, Little Red Riding Hood's mother gave her a pot of Brussels sprout soup.

Rules of
the Woods
1. Keep to
the path
2. Don't talk
to wolves

"Take this to your grandmother on the other side of the woods," she said.

"But remember the Rules of the Woods!"

8

"I promise,"
said Little Red
Riding Hood, and
off she went...

Skippety-skippety, skip. Skippety-skippety, skip.

"Oh what a
lovely day!"
said Little Red
Riding Hood.

"Good morning, Little Red Riding Hood,"
called the woodcutter.

"Good morning, Woodcutter," called Little Red Riding Hood.

Little Red Riding Hood walked deeper and deeper into the deep, dark woods.

It grew darker and darker.

So Little Red Riding Hood didn't see
the wolf waiting for her on the path.

And the wolf didn't see Little Red Riding Hood either.

13

Little Red Riding Hood
stumbled
straight
into the wolf.

Ow!

Argh!

Oof!

14

"What are you doing in the middle of the path?"
asked Little Red Riding Hood.
    "I nearly spilled my grandmother's Brussels sprout soup."

Sprouts! YUCK!
Wolves only eat
JUICY RED
MEAT!

Little Red Riding Hood had forgotten the rule
    —Don't talk to wolves.

The wolf was just about to gobble up
Little Red Riding Hood, when he had a BRILLIANT idea.

I'll eat Little Red Riding Hood

AND

her grandmother!

"And where does dear little Granny live?"
asked the wolf.

"In the cottage on the other side
of the woods," said Little Red Riding Hood.

The wolf raced to the cottage and knocked
on the door.

TAP!

TAP!

TAP!

"Come in,"
called Grandmother.

The wolf leaped into the room...

...and gobbled up Little Red Riding Hood's grandmother in two seconds flat.

Mmm! Bony, but not bad.

Then he pulled on her cap, jumped into bed and waited for Little Red Riding Hood.

Soon, there was a knock at the door.

TAP!   TAP!   TAP!   "Come in," snarled the wolf,
                          as softly as he could.

Little Red Riding Hood looked at her grandmother...

...then looked again.

In one bound, the wolf was out of bed and gobbling up Little Red Riding Hood. "Dee-licious!" he said...

...then fell fast asleep.

As he slept, he snored
– very **loudly**.

"What's going on?"
wondered the woodcutter.

"Oh no! I think he's eaten that poor old woman."
The woodcutter picked up some scissors.

He snipped open
the wolf's tummy.

Snippety-snip
Snippety-snip

Out popped Grandmother, and Little Red Riding Hood, too.

Quick as a flash, Little Red Riding Hood picked up some stones and piled them into the wolf's tummy.

When the wolf woke up, he tried to sneak out of the door.

RATTLE
RATTLE
RATTLE

But the stones rattled and rattled and rattled inside him.

"Now everyone can hear me coming.
I'll never catch anyone," cried the wolf.

"Exactly!" said the woodcutter.

"You'll just have to eat vegetables instead,"
said Little Red Riding Hood.

The wolf was never able
to eat another person.

Urgh! Brussels
sprout soup.

As for Little Red Riding Hood,
          she never, ever talked to a wolf again.

27

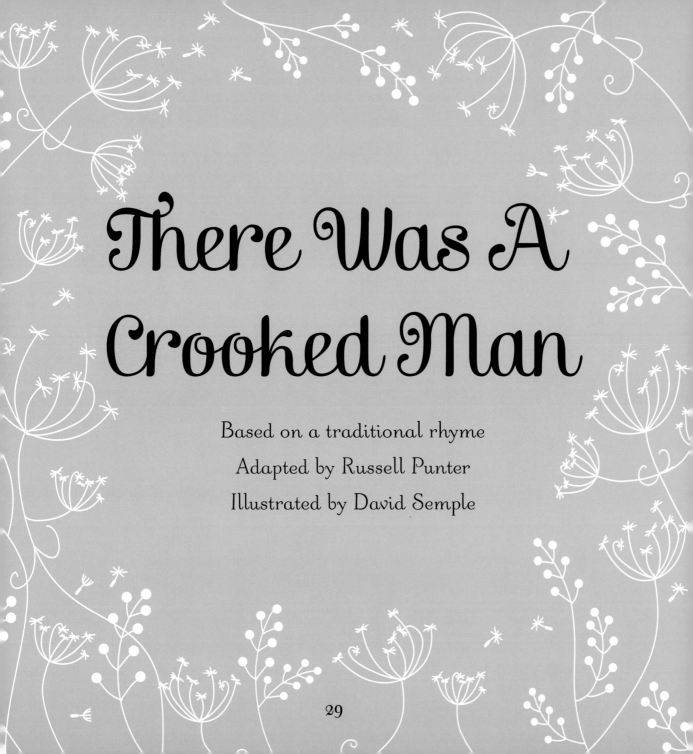

There Was A Crooked Man

Based on a traditional rhyme

Adapted by Russell Punter

Illustrated by David Semple

There was a crooked man

and he walked
a crooked mile.

He found a crooked sixpence,
upon a crooked stile.

He bought
a crooked cat

34

which caught a crooked mouse.

And they all lived together

in a little
crooked
house.

The crooked man
was hungry.

So he cooked
a crooked fish.

His crooked
cat could
smell it

and she snatched it
off the dish.

The crooked man was
angry.

He chased his cat outside.

He couldn't see her anywhere.

She'd found
a place to hide.

The man smelled something fishy,

so he followed
where it led...

across his crooked garden...

...into his crooked shed.

And there, behind a sack,

snuggled up against each other,

were thirteen hungry kittens

and their kind but crooked mother.

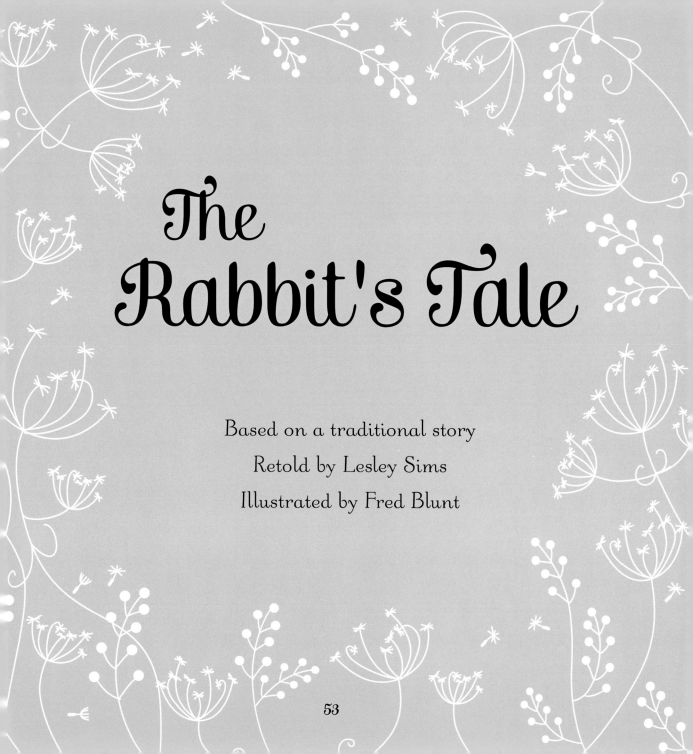

The Rabbit's Tale

Based on a traditional story

Retold by Lesley Sims

Illustrated by Fred Blunt

"My home is too small," sighed Rabbit, one day.
"I'm feeling all **squished** in."

"A rabbit needs space for flopping around
and dreaming of crunchy carrots."

"I know!" he decided.

"I'll go and see Owl.

He's wonderfully wise..."

"Tu-whit, tu-whoo.
What's the matter
with you?"

"My home is too
small. Please can
you help?"

57

Owl raised his eyes
to the sky.

"I've got it!" he cried, with a flap of his wings.
"Ask all your brothers and sisters to stay."

"Are you sure?" Rabbit said.

"I have quite a few..."

But off he hopped, up hills
and through fields, to ask
his family over.

61

They poured through the door,
with squeaks and with squeals...

...and munched through his carrots and cake.

"Oh dear!" Rabbit thought. "This won't do at all.
I can't even twitch my whiskers."

So he raced
back to Owl.

"Tu-whit, tu-whoo.
What's the matter with you?"

"I'm even more squashed
than before!"

"Dear me," said Owl, and thought for a while.
"Try asking your friends over too."

"How can that work?
Well, I'll give it
a whirl."

"Hello
Tortoise."

"Hello Mole."

"Please come to my
house for cake."

With a leap and a scamper, everyone came
and **squeezed** into Rabbit's house.

"Help!" thought Rabbit. "This can't be right.
I can hardly breathe."

He dashed back to Owl.

"Now there's NO room for me!"

"Then it's time for them all to leave."

71

Rabbit waved goodbye
as they left one by one.

"How's your house now, Rabbit?"

"There's so much space...
my home is HUGE!"

"Thank you Owl.
What a wise old
bird you are."

75

The Wind in the Willows

Based on the story by Kenneth Grahame

Retold by Lesley Sims

Illustrated by Mauro Evangelista

Ratty and Mole were out for a row,
just messing about on the river.

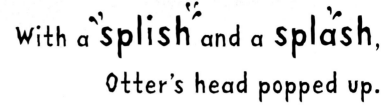

with a "**splish**" and a **splash**,
Otter's head popped up.

"Hello you two!" he gurgled.
"Toad is looking for you."

79

Toad Hall stood grand and tall, right on the edge of the river.

Ratty rowed there at once.

"You're here!" Toad cried. "Come for a ride in my brand new caravan."

They rambled along the country lanes, talking of this and of that.

Insects were humming and birds
were chirping, when...

Poop! Poop!

A sports car shot past in a cloud of
smoke, sending everyone flying.

82

"Scoundrels!" shouted Ratty.

"Villains!" muttered Mole.

"Poop! Poop!" said Toad. "Forget that boring old caravan. I'm buying a car."

From that moment, Toad was hooked.
Cars were all he could think about.

He drove them, he dreamed about
them and he cheered when
he saw a new one.

So Ratty and Mole amused themselves.
They played hide-and-seek in the
Wild Wood...

...or stayed with
their friend, Badger.

"How's Toad?" asked Badger one night, over cookies and cocoa. "Still buying new cars?"

"Buying them and crashing them," said
Ratty. "He's the World's Worst Driver."

"We'll have to help him," Badger declared.
"Tomorrow, we'll pay him a visit..."

"Hello you fellows!" said Toad, early the
next morning. "I'm just off for a drive."

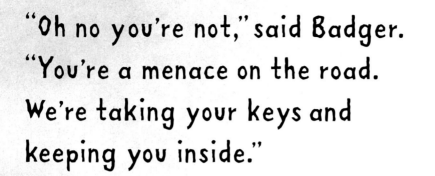

"Oh no you're not," said Badger.
"You're a menace on the road.
We're taking your keys and
keeping you inside."

"It's for your own
good, Toad," added Mole.

89

"They won't stop me!" Toad chuckled, as he escaped. "I'll find a car to drive."

Soon he saw the perfect one. As if in a dream, he clambered in... ...and sped away.

That night, Toad was in prison.
"Oh, why did I steal a car?"
he thought.

"Oh clever Badger, oh sensible Mole,
oh
foolish,
foolish
Toad."

Toad was down – but not for long.

Late one night, he escaped
from prison, cunningly
disguised as a
washerwoman.

When the moon was high in the sky,
he curled up by a tree and
snuggled into his shawl.

He fell asleep, dreaming of home.

But back at Toad Hall – calamity! His home had been stolen from him by stealthy stoats and wicked weasels.

"Don't panic, Toad," said Mole.
"Badger has a plan."

And Badger did, for he knew of a secret
tunnel that would take them right
into Toad Hall.

In the dead of night, armed with sticks and swords, they followed Badger down the secret tunnel...

...and burst out into the kitchen.

"CHARGE!" hollered Badger.

What a squealing and a screeching
filled the air.
"Take my house would you? Take that!"
shouted Toad.

The stoats and the weasels were banished forever. Toad was so thrilled, he held a small party to celebrate.

And he never drove another car again.

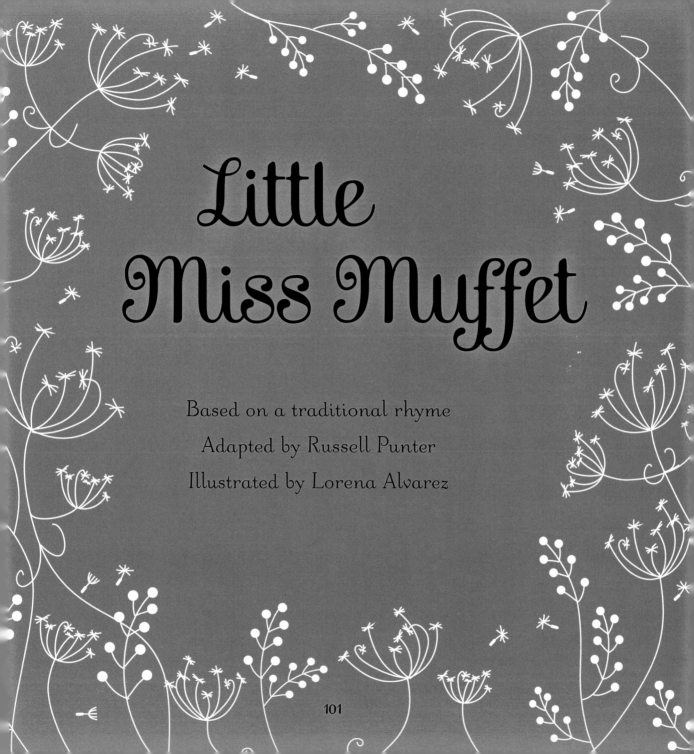

Little Miss Muffet

Based on a traditional rhyme

Adapted by Russell Punter

Illustrated by Lorena Alvarez

Little Miss Muffet
sat on a tuffet,

eating her curds
and whey.

Along came a spider,
who dropped down beside her,

and frightened Miss Muffet away.

"Help!" cried Miss Muffet.
She ran from her tuffet,
and into the woods
down below.

"Come back!" called the spider.

He rushed off to find her.

"I'm sorry for scaring you so."

The little girl sighed.
"What a bad place to hide.
Now I'm lost! I'll be stuck here all night."

Then she heard
a deep growl,

grrrrrr!

and an ear-splitting howl.

OWWWWOOOOO!

They gave poor
Miss Muffet a fright.

A big wolf jumped out.

He said with a shout,

"It's time for my dinner, my dear."

"I'll have
little girl pie!"

"Put her down!"
came a cry.

"Don't worry – Seb Spider is here."

The wolf gave
a smile.

"I do like
your style.

But what can you
do against me?"

"I'll show you," said Seb.

So he spun a strong web,

and tied the bad wolf
to a tree.

Miss Muffet said...

"Seb, what a wonderful web.

Now let's go!"

So Seb showed her the way.

Now she's
friends with
Seb Spider.

He hangs down
beside her,

and spins
    for Miss Muffet
        all day.

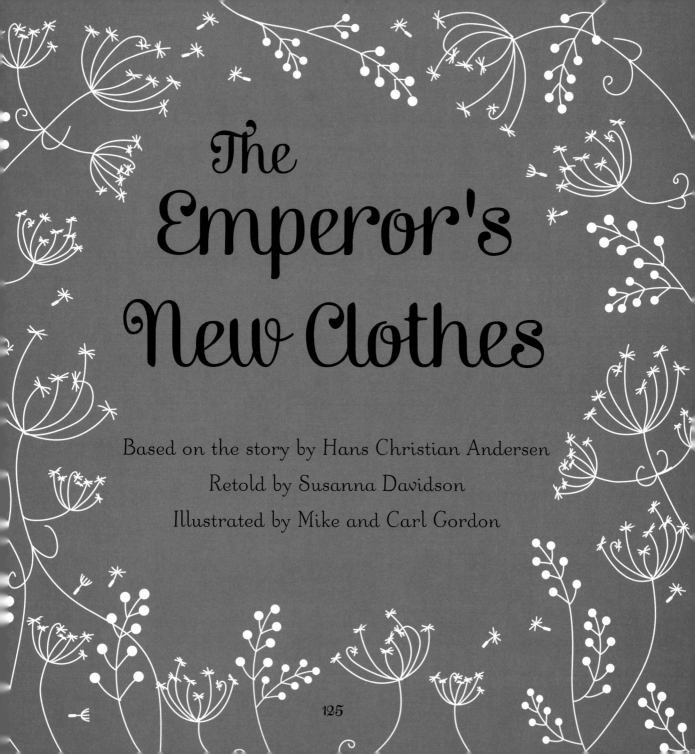

The
Emperor's
New Clothes

Based on the story by Hans Christian Andersen

Retold by Susanna Davidson

Illustrated by Mike and Carl Gordon

Once upon a time there was an
Emperor who loved clothes.

He liked looking splendid
ALL the time.

He had a different outfit for every day of the year.

But the Emperor had a problem.
He had nothing to wear for
the royal procession.

"Won't any of your outfits do,
Your Highness?" asked
his servant, Boris.

"NO!" said the Emperor. "I need a NEW outfit and I need one NOW."

"And remember – it has to be splendid."

Boris sighed and set off to find the finest clothes-makers in town.

WANTED!
Splendid new outfit for the Emperor.
Clothes-makers apply here!
NO TIME-WASTERS, PLEASE

He wasn't having much luck until...

130

a little round man

and a long thin man
rushed up to him.

They bowed with their
bottoms in the air.
"We are Slimus and
Slick, at your service,"
they said.

Boris took them to the Emperor.

"We make magic clothes," Slimus told him.
"Only clever people can see them. Stupid people can't!"

"Are they splendid?" asked the Emperor.
"Very splendid," promised Slick. "But very expensive.
We'll need pots and pots of money."

"Take all the money you want," cried the Emperor.
"Just make me those clothes!"

A week later, the Emperor and Boris went to see Slimus and Slick at work. "Welcome!" they said. "What do you think of our clothes?"

The Emperor gulped. Boris gulped. Neither of them could see a thing.

But they didn't want to look stupid.
So the Emperor said, "Splendid!"
"Yes, really very... splendid," said Boris.

"Oh, um, er, most splendid!" added the footmen.

Here! Have more money.

As soon as everyone had gone, Slimus and Slick laughed and laughed until their faces turned purple.

Then they ordered a huge feast.
"It's hungry work making magic clothes," they said.

On the morning of the
royal procession, the Emperor
couldn't wait to put on his new clothes.

"Here is your cloak," said Slimus.
"It's light as a feather."

"Oh Your Highness," said Slick. "You look
very handsome. Your clothes fit so well."

139

The Emperor admired himself in the mirror. "Don't I look **splendid?**"

"Yes, Your *Highness,*" gasped the footmen, staring straight at the Emperor.

"Yes, Your Highness," said Boris, staring straight at the ceiling. (He was trying NOT to look.)

"Open the palace gates!" ordered the Emperor.
"Let the royal procession begin."

The crowd gasped
when they saw the Emperor.
Everyone had heard that only
clever people could see his clothes.

"Aren't his clothes *splendid?*" they said.

"Let me see him!" called a small boy, who was stuck at the back of the crowd.

"Ooh!" said the boy. "The Emperor's got no clothes on!"

Faster than a spreading fire,
a whisper whizzed
through the crowd.

145

The Emperor heard their words. He looked down.
"Oh no," he thought. "I'm naked!"

Then he blushed
bright red.

"But I can't stop now. This is the royal procession and I am the Emperor."
So he held his head high and walked on.

The crowd clapped and cheered. They thought it was the most splendid royal procession ever!

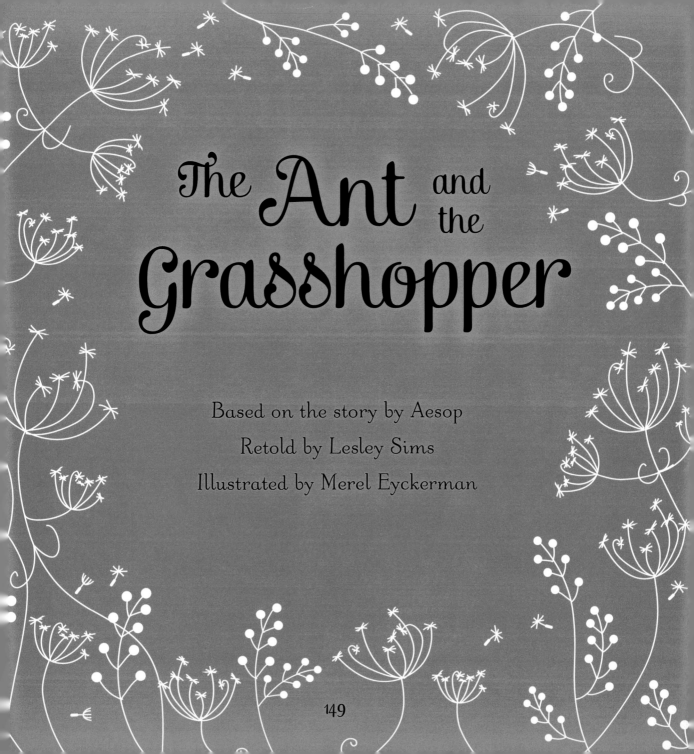

The Ant and the Grasshopper

Based on the story by Aesop

Retold by Lesley Sims

Illustrated by Merel Eyckerman

It was a glorious summer's day.
Grasshopper chirruped and
sang sunny songs.

151

Ant was too busy to sing.
He huffed...
...and he puffed...
...and he g-r-o-a-n-e-d...

as he hauled food away
to his winter store.

Grasshopper smiled and
lay back on a leaf, drowsy
and dozing in the sun.

After a while, he called out to Ant,
"You're working too hard!"

"I have to,"
Ant panted.
"There's so much to do."

"I must collect
all this food
for the winter."

"But winter is ages away,"
said Grasshopper.

"Enjoy the sunshine
with me while you can!"

"Winter may seem ages away," Ant replied,
"but it will come all too swiftly."

"If you don't work now...

　　...why, when the Sun has long gone and the Earth
　　is sleeping, you will be cold and hungry."

Grasshopper laughed and sang on.

Ant huffed...
and he puffed...
and carried more corn.

Sure enough, winter crept over the Earth.
Trees stood bare against the bleak sky.
Snow dusted the fields.

Tucked up snug in his
little home, Ant looked at
his food store and smiled.

He had boxes galore, plenty to keep him fed
until the spring buds blossomed.

165

Outside, in a blustery gale,
Grasshopper scrunched himself up,
trying to shelter behind a leaf.

But the wind blew through his
trembling body, however tightly he curled.
His tummy ached with hunger.

At last, he fought through the wind to Ant's house. "Ant! Help!" Grasshopper shouted.

Ant poked his head outside his door.

"Grasshopper! You look frozen," he cried.
"Come inside and get warm."

"Thaw out by the stove," said Ant, "and I'll make supper."

170

Grasshopper beamed.
He could almost taste
the toasted corn already.

"Thank you kind, clever Ant,"
he said, basking in the heat of the flames.
"I promise, next summer, I'll work too!"

171

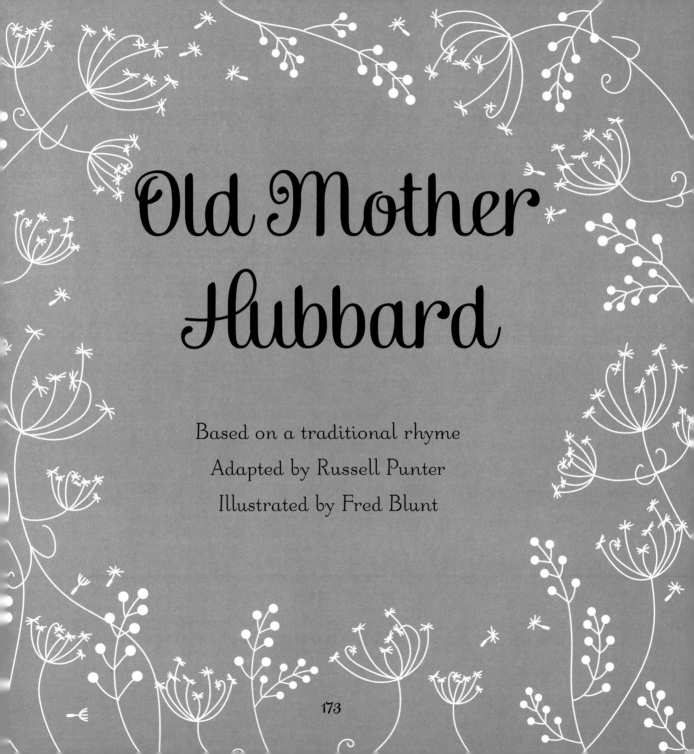

Old Mother Hubbard

Based on a traditional rhyme

Adapted by Russell Punter

Illustrated by Fred Blunt

Old Mother
Hubbard
went to
the cupboard,

to fetch her poor doggie a bone.

175

But when she got there...

the cupboard was BARE!

And so the poor doggie had none.

Old Mother Hubbard

shut up the cupboard

...and put on her warm winter clothes.

"We'll have to
go out,"

she said with
a shout,

"before all the
butchers are
closed."

So off down the lane,

through wind
and through
rain,

went Old Mother Hubbard
and Spot.

'Til they came to a stop at Bob's Butcher's Shop.

And they went in to see what was what.

b the Butcher

There was plenty of meat,
for a doggie-sized treat,

but the old lady picked out a bone.

Then came the snag, when she looked in her bag –

she had left all her money at home.

The pair stepped outside.

"Stop thief!" came Bob's cry.

Bob the Butcher

And a man hurried by in a flash.

He ran with such speed,

he tripped on Spot's lead.

And went **flying**, along with the cash.

"Your dog stopped that thief," said Bob with relief.

"So I must reward you, my dear."

Now Old Mother
Hubbard has a
very full cupboard,

and her dog has the
best steak all year.

The Three Little Pigs

Based on a traditional story

Retold by Susanna Davidson

Illustrated by Georgien Overwater

Once upon a time,
there were three little pigs.

They lived with their mother in a snug little house...

until the little pigs grew **too big**.

"It's time you found homes of your own,"
said their mother.

So off they trotted, on their short pink legs.

Trottity-trot,

trottity-trot,

trottity-trot.

"Watch out for the big bad wolf,"
called Mother Pig.

Soon, they met a man selling straw.

"Ooh!" squealed the first little pig.
"May I buy some?"

"I'm going to build
a straw house."

He set to work right away.

His house had four straw walls,

a neat straw floor,

a fine straw roof,

and a
stylish
straw
door.

"Isn't it grand?" said the first little pig.
The others weren't *so* sure.
They muttered and tutted, then trotted away.

Soon, they met a man selling sticks.

"Ooh!" squealed the second little pig. "May I buy some?"

"I'm going to build a stick house," he said proudly.

"Isn't my house grand?
Sticks are better than straw."

The third little pig
wasn't so sure.

She trotted on, until...

Bricks
for sale

Bricks
for sale

...she found some bricks.

BUY
BRICKS
HERE

"Ooh! Please may I buy
some?" she asked.
"I'm going to build
a brick house."

Bricks
for sale

204

"Brick houses are the best of all."

The next day, the big bad wolf
came to the straw house.
"Little pig, little pig, let me in!"
he called.

"Not by the hair on
my chinny chin chin,"
said the first little pig.

"Then I'll **huff** and
I'll **puff** and I'll
BLOW your house in."

The little pig ran as fast as he could to the stick house. The wolf was right behind him.

"Little pigs, little pigs, let me in!" cried the wolf.

"Not by the hair
on our chinny chin chins!"
cried the two little pigs.

"Then I'll **huff** and I'll **puff** and I'll BLOW your house in."

And he **huffed**...

and he **puffed**...

...until, at last, he BLEW the house in.

The little pigs ran as fast as they could to the brick house.
The wolf was just behind them.

"Little pigs, little pigs, let me in!"

"No!" yelled the three little pigs.
"Not by the hair on our chinny chin chins!"

"Then I'll **huff** and I'll **puff** and I'll BLOW your house in!" cried the wolf.

And he **huffed** and he **puffed** and he **huffed** and he **puffed**.

214

He **huffed**
and he
puffed
until...

Puff

Huff

...he ran out of **puff**.

"Hee, hee, hee!" laughed
the three little pigs.
"You can't get in!"

But the wolf jumped onto the roof.

He slid down the chimney

and landed

SPLOSH!

in the cooking pot.

The third little pig picked up the lid...

...and all three slammed it on.

"By the hair on our chinny chin chins," they said, "we won't be seeing that wolf again!"

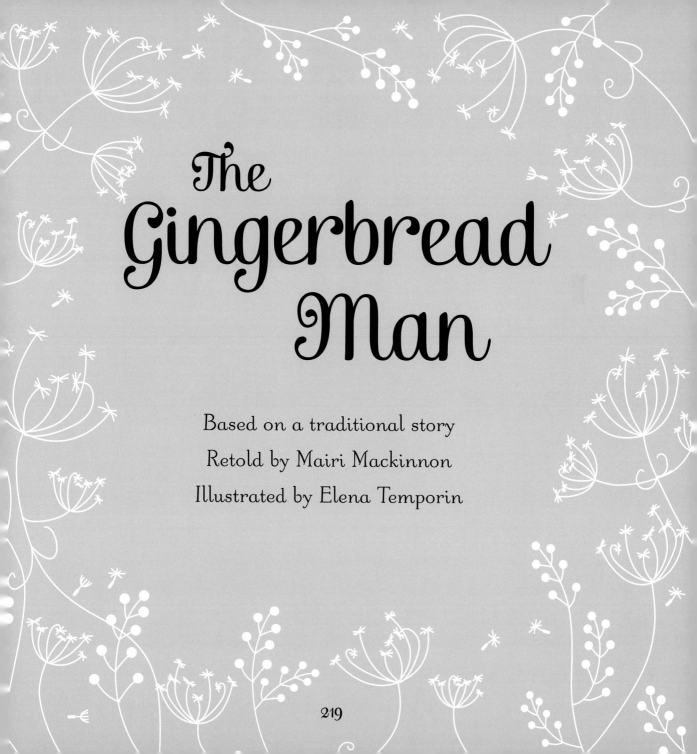

The Gingerbread Man

Based on a traditional story

Retold by Mairi Mackinnon

Illustrated by Elena Temporin

Once upon a time, many years ago,

a little old woman

and a little old man
    lived on a farm.

221

They were kind people.
It made them sad that
they had no children.

"If only we had a little boy," sighed the old woman.

So she took out her recipe book.

She weighed and she measured,

she mixed and
she stirred,

she rolled the dough
and she cut out a shape.

Then she put it in the oven to bake.

225

Soon the kitchen was filled with the smell of hot gingerbread.

"Almost ready now," said the old woman,
and opened the oven to look.

Mmmm...

Out jumped a little gingerbread man!

He pattered across
the kitchen floor...

...and ran right out
of the open door!

"Stop!" called the old woman.

"Stop, stop!" called the old man.

But the gingerbread man
ran along the road, singing:

Run, run, as fast as you can,

You can't catch me,

I'm the gingerbread man!

He raced past a horse
and a cow, grazing in the meadow.

"Mmm, you look delicious," neighed the horse.

"Come here, little man," mooed the cow.

But the gingerbread man ran along the road, singing:

I have run away from a little old woman and a little old man,
and I can run away from you too, yes I can!

Run, run, as fast as you can,
You can't catch me,
I'm the gingerbread man!

He sped past a farmer,
hard at work in a field.

"Mmm, what a treat,"
said the farmer.
"Come here, little man."

But the gingerbread man ran along the road, singing:

I have run away from a horse, a cow,

a little old woman and a little old man,

and I can run away from you too, yes I can!

Run, run, as fast as you can,

You can't catch me,

I'm the gingerbread man!

He scampered past a school,

and all the children shouted,
"Mmm, we love gingerbread!
Come here, little man!"

But the gingerbread man ran along the road, singing:

I have run away from a farmer in a field, a horse, a cow,
a little old woman and a little old man,

and I can run away from you too, yes I can!

Run, run, as fast as you can,

You can't catch me,

I'm the gingerbread man!

On and on he ran,
until he came to a river.

He wanted to cross it,
but he was afraid
of getting wet.

A fox spotted him.
"If you climb onto
my tail, I'll help you
across," he said.

The fox started swimming with the
gingerbread man on his tail.

Soon, though, his tail was dragging in the water.

"I'm so sorry," said the fox.

"Do climb onto my back."

But soon the water was lapping over the fox's back.

"I'm so sorry," said the fox.
"Do climb onto my head."

The gingerbread man tiptoed
up to the fox's head...

The fox tossed his head, and SNAP!
The gingerbread man was a quarter gone.

SNAP!
He was half gone.

SNAP!
Three quarters gone...

SNAP! And that was the end of him.

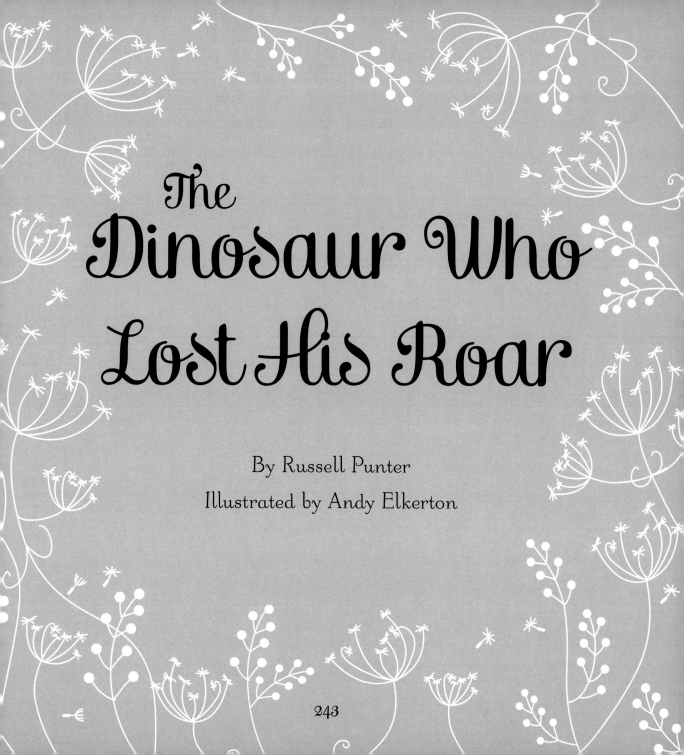

The Dinosaur Who Lost His Roar

By Russell Punter

Illustrated by Andy Elkerton

Deep inside the forest,
lived a dinosaur named Sid.

ROAR!

He always got in trouble
for the noisy things he did.

Spike was picking berries,

Sid crept up like a cat.

He let out such a mighty

ROAR!

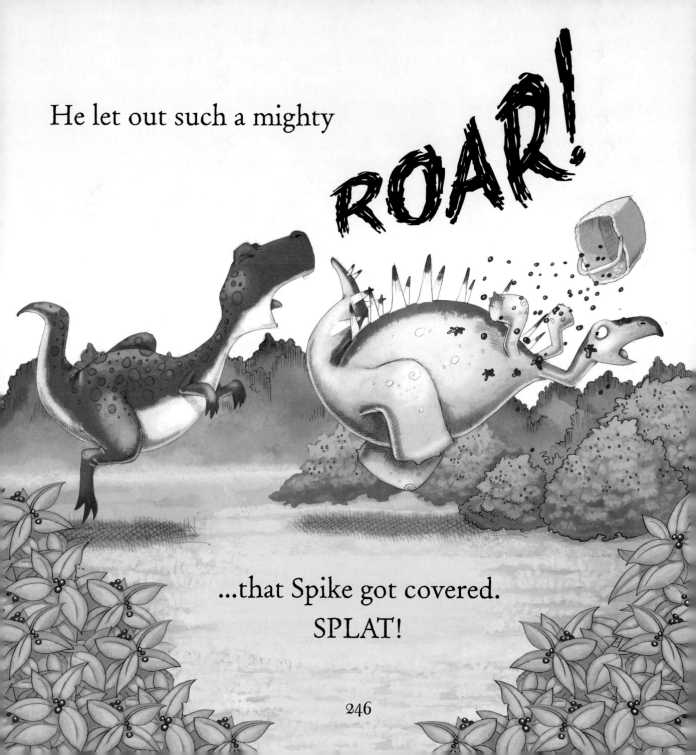

...that Spike got covered.
SPLAT!

"That wasn't funny, Sid," growled Spike.

"The juice went in my eyes."

"Enjoy your breakfast!" Sid replied.
"Who else can I surprise?"

Ross was standing by the pool
to see what he could catch.

When Sid let out a mighty

ROAR!

...poor Ross went tumbling. SPLASH!

"I hope you liked your swim, Ross.
You'll dry out in the end."

"That wasn't funny,"
Ross replied.

"I thought you
were my friend."

Sid saw Ellie hunting eggs.
He sneaked behind her back.

He let out such a mighty

ROAR!

...the eggs went
flying. CRACK!

"An eggs-ellent surprise," laughed Sid.
"You just can't beat my roar."

But when he went to bed that night,
his throat felt rough and sore.

The next day, Sid saw Spike again
and went to play his joke.

But when he tried to give a roar,
what came out
was a...

croak!

"Ha ha, Sid. You've lost your roar.
You can't scare me any more."

Ross was balanced on a rock. Sid went to scare him off.
But when he tried to give a roar,
what came out
was a...

cough!

"Ha ha, Sid. You've lost your roar.
You can't scare me any more."

Sid tiptoed up to Ellie,
but struggle though he might,

no roar would come out
– just a rasp...

His throat felt oh-so tight.

raaasssp!

"Ha ha, Sid. You've lost your roar.
You can't scare me any more."

Sid spent a whole week
getting well,

with honey
and sweet tea.

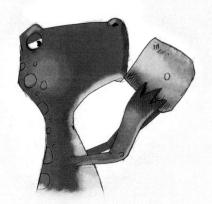

"Oh, I wish I hadn't
played those tricks.

Now the joke's on me."

Soon Sid felt fit
to see his friends.

"I'll show them
I'm not mean."

But when he reached
the berry bush,
Spike could not be seen.

Ross was missing
from his pool,

Sid sensed that things weren't right.

He spotted scary footprints
and they gave him quite a fright.

Sid was getting worried.

What would he come to next?

Then came a shock, beyond a rock –

Tyrannosaurus Rex!

Sid hoped he had his voice back.
But how could he be sure?

He took the most enormous breath,
and gave a mighty...

The T-Rex headed for the hills.
Sid's pals were safe once more.

"Three cheers for Sid the hero,

You're the greatest dinosaur!"

Goldilocks
and the
Three Bears

Based on a traditional story

Retold by Susanna Davidson

Illustrated by Mike and Carl Gordon

Once upon a time, there was a little girl called...

GOLDILOCKS!

She liked to do something naughty each day.

MONDAY...

TUESDAY...

WEDNESDAY... Goldi

THURSDAY...

"Now..." thought Goldilocks. "What shall I do next?"

Goldilocks' mother always said, "Don't go into the forest. It's full of big, scary bears."

BEWARE OF THE BEARS!

But Goldilocks wasn't scared.
So on Friday, she went
into the forest.

"Ha!" she said. "I can't see any bears."
She skipped happily along the path
until she saw...

271

...a pretty little cottage.

"I wonder who lives here?" thought Goldilocks, and went inside.

Bear Cottage

"Mmm..." she said.
On the table were three
delicious-smelling bowls of porridge.

"I'm sure no one would mind if I had a tiny taste,"
thought Goldilocks.

273

First, Goldilocks tried the great, big bowl.

Next, she tried the middle-sized bowl.

OW!
too hot!

Last of all, Goldilocks
tried the tiny bowl.

"Yum! Yum!" she said.
"Just right!"

And she ate it ALL up.

Feeling full, Goldilocks
looked for somewhere to sit.

First, she tried
the great, big chair.

Next, she tried the
middle-sized chair.

Last of all,
she tried the tiny chair.

"Aha!" thought Goldilocks.
"Just right." Until...

CRACK!

The chair broke.

"Oops!" said Goldilocks. "Time for a nap."

Upstairs, she found a great, big bed.

Too hard!

Next, she tried the middle-sized bed.

Too soft!

Last of all, she tried the tiny bed.
"Just right," said Goldilocks,
snuggling down.

Snore! Snore! Snore!

As she slept, a large paw pulled open the front door.

Three bears plodded into the house.

There was...

a great big father bear,

a middle-sized mother bear

and a tiny little baby bear.

"Who's been eating *my* porridge?"
growled Father Bear.

"Who's been eating *my* porridge?"
howled Mother Bear.

"Who's been eating *my* porridge?"
squeaked Baby Bear.

They've eaten it all up!

Father Bear looked
around the room.

"Who's been sitting in
my chair?" he growled.

"Well! Who's been
sitting in *my* chair?"
howled Mother Bear.

"Who's been sitting in *my* chair?"
squeaked Baby Bear.

"They've broken it!"

They
heard
a rumbling
((**snore**))
coming
from
the
bedroom.

The three bears
climbed the
stairs.

"Who's been sleeping in *my* bed?" growled Father Bear.

"Who's been sleeping in *my* bed?"
howled Mother Bear.

"Who's been sleeping in *my* bed?"
squeaked Baby Bear.

"She's still there!"

Goldilocks woke up and
SCREAMED!

She flew out of the cottage and ran all the way home, crying...

"I'll NEVER, EVER be naughty again."

The Owl and the Pussy-cat

By Edward Lear

Illustrated by Victoria Ball

The Owl and the Pussy-cat
went to sea
in a beautiful
pea-green boat.

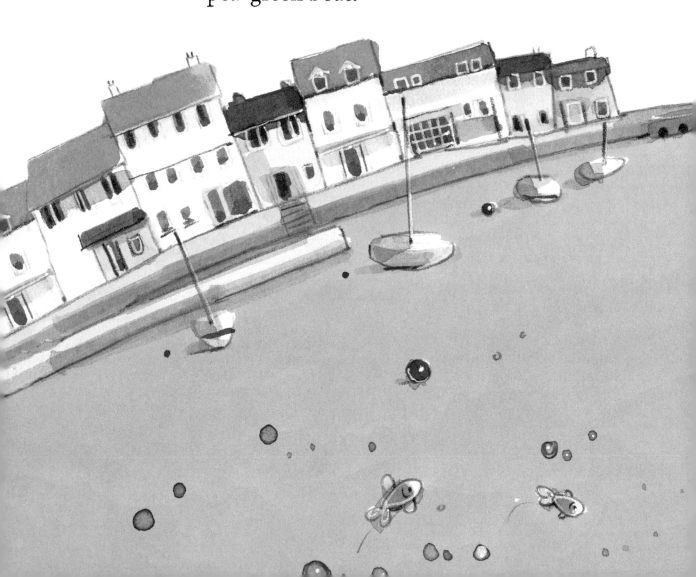

They took some honey, and plenty of money,
wrapped up in a five-pound note.

The Owl looked up
to the stars above,
and sang to a small guitar.

"O lovely Pussy! O Pussy, my love,
What a beautiful Pussy you are, you are, you are!

What a beautiful
Pussy you are!"

Pussy said to the Owl,
"You elegant fowl,

how charmingly
sweet you sing."

"Oh let us be married – too long we have tarried.

But what shall we do for a ring?"

They sailed away...

...for a year and a day...

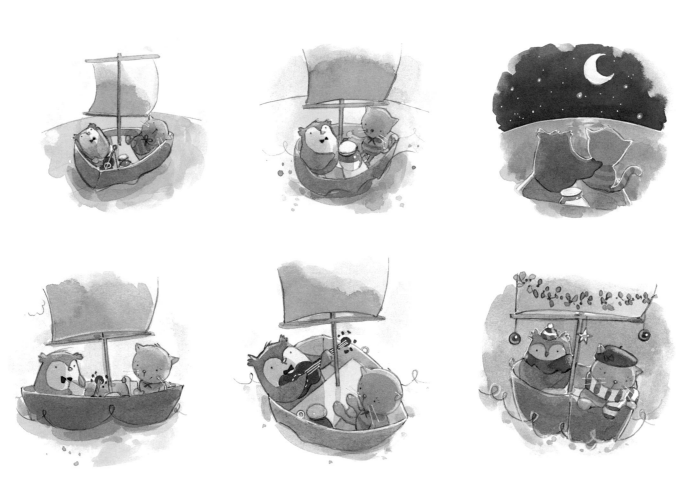

...to the land where the Bong-tree grows.

And there in a wood a Piggy-wig stood,
with a ring at the end of his nose,
his nose, his nose,

with a ring at the
end of his nose.

"Dear Pig,
are you willing,

to sell for one shilling,
your ring?"

Said the Piggy, "I will!"

So they took it away,

and were married
next day,

by the Turkey who
lives on the hill.

They dined on mince,
   and slices of quince,

               which they ate with a runcible spoon.

And hand in hand,
on the edge of the sand,

they danced by the light of the moon, the moon, the moon,
they danced by the light of the moon.

The Reluctant Dragon

Based on the story by Kenneth Grahame

Retold by Lesley Sims

Illustrated by Fred Blunt

Aaargh!

One summer's evening,
a shepherd tore down the hill to
his cottage. **"Aaargh!"** he screamed.

He flung open the door.

"I... just... saw... a... dragon," he panted.

"A **dragon?**"
shrieked his wife.

"A **dragon!**" thought their son, Sam.

"I wonder if he's friendly?"

The next morning, Sam set off to find out.

"I'll be extra careful,"
he promised his parents.
"At the first sign of smoke, I'll run!"

But the dragon **was** friendly - and he was thrilled to see Sam.

"I love my cave, but it does get lonely," he said.

The dragon told tales of long, long ago.

Once upon a time,
fire-breathing dragons
filled the skies.

They kidnapped princesses
and battled bold knights.

The dragon loved telling stories
and Sam loved hearing them.
Every day, he came back for more, until...

318

...the villagers found out about the dragon. They were terrified. They trembled in their tunics and quaked in their boots.

We need someone to fight this monster!

Sam raced off to warn him.

"The villagers want to get rid of you!" he gasped. "They say you're **dangerous**."

Nonsense! I wouldn't hurt a fly!

That afternoon, Sam
heard even worse news.

Look! It's Saint
George, the
dragon killer!

Oh no!

Hurray!

Sam rushed back to the dragon.

321

"Saint George has come to fight you," Sam shouted.
"And he has the longest, **pointiest** spear I've ever seen."

"But I don't like fighting," said
the dragon. "I'll hide in my
cave until he goes."

"You can't," said Sam. "He'll find you."

The dragon yawned.
"I'm sure you'll think of
something," he drawled.

Sam wandered through the village square,
thinking hard.

A crowd was telling Saint George
about the dastardly dragon.

He'll eat us all!

He'll set us on fire!

When the villagers had gone, Sam went up to Saint George. "It's not true!" he protested. "The dragon wouldn't hurt a fly."

"But they want me to fight him," said Saint George. "What can I do?"

"I've got an idea," Sam said. "Come and meet the dragon."

"Here's the plan," said Sam.
"You could have a pretend fight."

"But it must look real," insisted Saint George.

And then we can have a feast!

Mmm...

The next day, Sam waited nervously by the dragon's cave.

The entire village trekked up the hill to watch the fight.

Colossal cheers broke out when Saint George rode into view.

But **where** was the dragon?

A roar echoed around the hills.
Flames blistered the air
and the dragon
thundered out of his cave.

"**Charge!**" yelled Saint
George, galloping forward.

The dragon bounded up...

...and they shot past
each other, with a wink.

"Missed!"
cried the crowd.

Saint George and the
dragon swung around and
charged again.

CLATTER! BANG! OOF!

The dragon gave a groan and slumped
to the ground. Saint George stood
over him in triumph.

"I think the dragon has learned
his lesson," declared Saint George.
"Let's invite him to our feast."

And he led the villagers,
Sam and the dragon
down the hill.

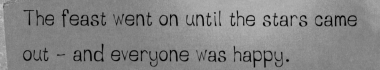

The feast went on until the stars came
out – and everyone was happy.

Sam was happy because his plan had worked.

The villagers were
happy because they'd
seen a fight.

Saint George was happy because he'd won.

But the dragon was happiest of all,
for he had lots of new friends...

...and a very full tummy.

The Story of Pinocchio

Based on the story by Carlo Collodi

Retold by Katie Daynes

Illustrated by Mauro Evangelista

Gepetto the carpenter had always wanted to make a puppet. One day, he found the perfect piece of wood.

He began by carving a head and a little nose.

Slowly, the nose grew...

longer...

and longer...

and longer.

Gepetto was astonished, but he carried on carving.

Hours later, he finished his long-nosed puppet and smiled.

Suddenly, the puppet jumped up, snatched
Gepetto's wig and ran outside.

"Come back here, puppet!"
Gepetto cried.

"I'm not a puppet," shouted the
puppet. "My name is Pinocchio
and I'm a real boy."

Pinocchio kept running,
straight past
a policeman.

"What's going on?" asked the policeman.
Then he saw Gepetto waving a chisel.
"Stop there, old man," he ordered. "You look dangerous."

341

"Tee hee," giggled
Pinocchio. He skipped
back home and snuggled
in an armchair by the fire.

BuzzzzzzzzzzzzzZZZzz

"Foolish puppet,"
buzzed a cricket.

"Hey!" shouted Pinocchio.
"I'm not a puppet. I'm a real boy."

"Oh no you're not," said
the cricket. "You're
a naughty puppet.
Only good puppets
become real boys."

Pinocchio was lost in thought...

until Gepetto arrived home with some supper.

"Er... Dad," said Pinocchio.
"I want to be a real boy."

Gepetto smiled.
"Well let's start by
sending you to school."

Be good, Pinocchio!

On the way to school, Pinocchio saw a crowd of people.

"Are you here for the puppet show?" asked a well-dressed man.

"A puppet show?"
said Pinocchio. "Oh yes!"

He sold his school book,
bought a ticket...

...and dashed
into the show.

"Hello puppet," the performers called to
Pinocchio. "Come and join us."

"We're going to the Land of Lost Toys," said a clown. "Do you want to come along?"

"I'd love to!" replied Pinocchio at once.

The Land of Lost Toys was one big funfair.

"Yippeeeeee!" squealed Pinocchio.

"Are you a lost toy too?"
asked a teddy bear.

"Um... yes," lied Pinocchio.
His wooden nose began to itch.

"I have no family," said the teddy bear.
"Nor do I," lied Pinocchio.

His itchy nose began to grow.

It grew

longer

and *longer*.

"Foolish puppet,"
buzzed a voice.
"Your poor father
is sick with worry.
He's rowing across
the ocean, searching for you."

"Oh no," Pinocchio sighed. "I must
find him." Instantly, his nose began to shrink.

"I'll help," cooed a pigeon.

Pinocchio jumped on her back
and they soared to the coast.

Pinocchio?
Where are you?

"There he is!"
cried Pinocchio.

As the puppet watched, a **huge** wave

rose up and swallowed Gepetto's boat.

"I'll save you, Dad!"
cried Pinocchio, diving
into the chilly sea.

Pinocchio swam and swam... but there was no sign of Gepetto.

Then he felt a rush of water
and everything went dark.

"Where am I?" wondered Pinocchio, with a shudder.
Peering into the gloom, he saw a faint glow.

He followed it down a squelchy tunnel...

SQUELCH

SQUELCH

...and stopped in surprise.

An old man was sitting at a desk.
  "Dad?" whispered Pinocchio.

Pinocchio!

"I'm sorry I was so naughty," said Pinocchio.
                    "But don't worry, I'll get us out of here."

357

Pinocchio led Gepetto back along the dark, squelchy tunnel, to the mouth of a cave.

"Jump!" cried Pinocchio. "I'll tow you to the shore."

By midnight, Pinocchio and Gepetto were safely home.
"You're a good puppet," said Gepetto, kissing his son goodnight.

The next morning, Pinocchio woke up
feeling very different.

"Dad!" he
shouted. "I'm a
real boy at last."

Edited by Jenny Tyler and Lesley Sims

Designed by Caroline Spatz

Additional design: Louise Flutter, Hannah Ahmed,
Andrea Slane and Katarina Dragoslavic

Digital manipulation: Nick Wakeford and Mike Wheatley

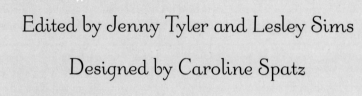

First published in 2013 by Usborne Publishing Ltd.,
Usborne House, 83-85 Saffron Hill, London EC1N 8RT, England.
www.usborne.com Copyright © 2013 Usborne Publishing Ltd.